701

OCT 2 5 2007

ALLEN COUNTY PUBLIC LIBRARY

3 1833 05540

FRIENDS
OF ACPL

It's Christmas

TINA BURKE

Kane/Miller
BOOK PUBLISHERS

ALLEN COUNTY PUBLIC LIBRARY

Kane/Miller Book Publishers, Inc.
First American Edition 2007
by Kane/Miller Book Publishers, Inc.
La Jolla, California

First published by Penguin Group (Australia), 2006
Copyright © Tina Burke, 2006

All rights reserved. For information contact:
Kane/Miller Book Publishers, Inc.
P.O. Box 8515
La Jolla, CA 92038
www.kanemiller.com

Library of Congress Control Number: 2007921047
Printed and bound in China
1 2 3 4 5 6 7 8 9 10

ISBN: 978-1-933605-44-9

To Mum, Dad, Paul and Sean… Merry Christmas!

It’s that time of year again.

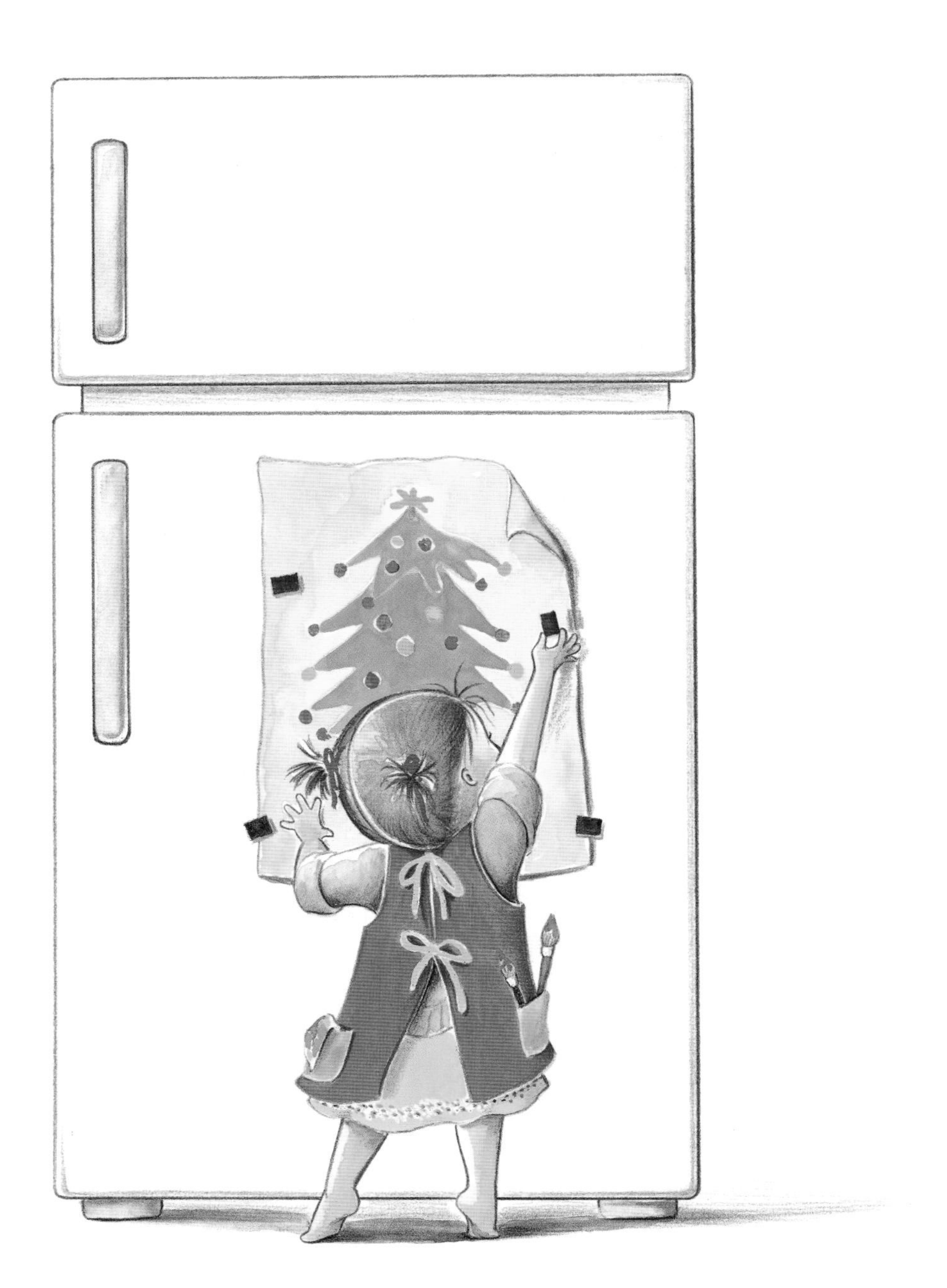

There are things to do…

. . . and people to see.

There are carols to sing…

. . . and decorations to make.

(Of course, some people get a little more into the spirit than others.)

The tree must be trimmed…

. . . and the perfect gift
must be bought,

$100
$150
$100

or made.

for
Mum

Sometimes it's nice to have
a special memento.

Stockings are placed where
Santa will find them,

and perhaps a little snack.

for
Santa

And all that is left to do

is wait…

for
Santa

and wait…

MERRY CHRISTMAS